Mairi's Mermaid

EGMONT
We bring stories to life

Book Band: Turquoise

First published in Great Britain 2001
This Reading Ladder edition published 2016
by Egmont UK Limited
The Yellow Building, 1 Nicholas Road, London W11 4AN
Text copyright © Michael Morpurgo 1994
Illustrations copyright © Lucy Richards 2001
The author and illustrator have asserted their moral rights
ISBN 978 1 4052 8201 7
www.egmont.co.uk
A CIP catalogue record for this title is available from the British Library.
Printed in Singapore
30983/24

Series consultant: Nikki Gamble

MIX
Paper
FSC FSC® C018306

Mairi's Mermaid

Michael Morpurgo

Illustrated by Lucy Richards

Reading Ladder

For Alan
M.M.

For Grandad Eric
and all my family
L.R.

Mairi still could not swim. She wished she could, but she just couldn't.

All the holidays she'd been trying, but every time she took her feet off the bottom she sank like a stone.

Her brother Robbie swam like a fish.

'It's easy,' he told her. 'You believe in

mermaids don't you? Well, just pretend

you're a mermaid, like this.'

He doesn't even have armbands.

He laughed and plunged headfirst into
another towering green wave. Sometimes
Robbie was a real show-off.

Mairi's mother and father tried to help.

'It'll come' they said. 'You'll do it.'

But it didn't come and she didn't do it.

Mairi wanted to be miserable all

on her own.

She went to look for crabs in the rock pools and tried to forget all about swimming.

Soon she had collected five little crabs in her bucket. They'd be her pets for the day. Later she'd let them go and watch them sidle away into the sea.

The water in the rock pool was warm from the sun. A shoal of silver fish darted round her legs. She could see a starfish and some sea anemones. 'Swimming looks so easy for them,' she thought.

That's a funny looking fish!

10

Suddenly something pinched her toe. She thought it might be a crab and jumped up. It was nothing. Maybe she had imagined it. But just to be sure, she decided not to dangle her feet again.

And then she heard a piping voice. It
seemed at first to come from far away.
She listened again. It came from deep
down in the rock pool.

Mairi brushed aside the seaweed and there, glaring up at her, was a huge brown crab. In his great grasping claw was a fish, no bigger than her finger.

But then she saw it wasn't an ordinary
fish. It was a fish with arms and hands,
a fish with a head like her own and a
mouth that spoke. It was a little
mermaid.

Help!

Mairi was not at all afraid of crabs, however big they were. She picked the crab out of the water and shook him and shook him.

The little mermaid dropped into the pool and disappeared.

For a moment there was no sign of her.

Then a small head bobbed up. 'Thank

you, oh, thank you,' the mermaid said.

Mairi never knew mermaids could be this small. She wasn't sure mermaids were even real.

'Help me, please,' said the mermaid.
'I went off on my own and I got stuck in
this pool. Then that great big horrible crab
caught me. He was going to eat me up!'

Of course I'm real!

Mairi would *so* like to have kept her as
a pet for the day, but she knew what she
had to do.

Mairi carried the little mermaid carefully over the rocks and down to the sea. Then she opened her hands, and let the mermaid go. But the mermaid wouldn't go.

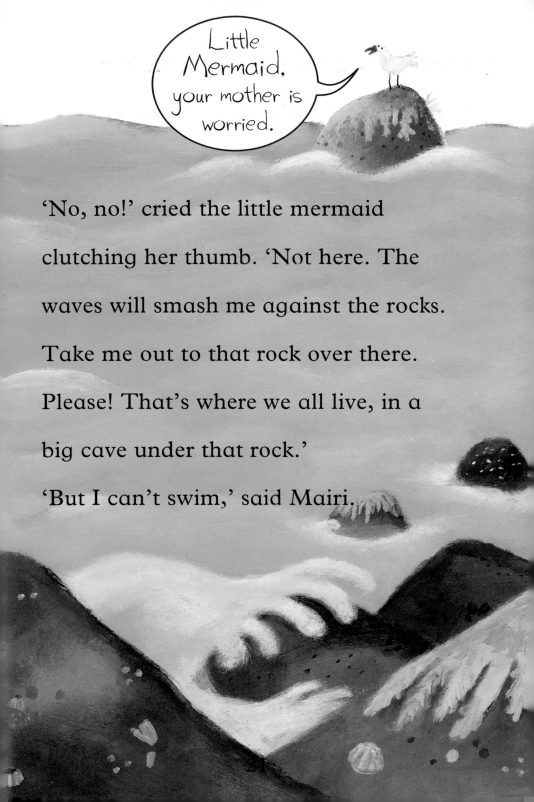

'Little Mermaid, your mother is worried.'

'No, no!' cried the little mermaid clutching her thumb. 'Not here. The waves will smash me against the rocks. Take me out to that rock over there. Please! That's where we all live, in a big cave under that rock.'

'But I can't swim,' said Mairi.

21

'I'll tell you what,' Mairi said. 'I'll take you as far as I can walk, but I can't go out of my depth.'

She stepped into the sea and waded out until the sea water came as high as her knees . . .

as high as her waist . . .

as high as her neck . . .

Suddenly a great wave came rolling in and lifted her right off her feet and when she came down there was no sandy bottom under her feet, no bottom at all.

Mairi kicked and splashed and the seawater came right into her mouth.

'It's all right,' said the little mermaid.

'You're swimming!'

And when Mairi kicked again, she did

not sink. She was swimming! She was!

I'm not sinking!

She lifted her chin and paddled through
the sea, keeping her mouth tightly closed.
Together, Mairi and the little mermaid
swam to the rock.

You're swimming!

Not bad, for someone with only two legs.

Home safe and sound.

They were almost there when Mairi felt an arm around her waist, then another and another. The sea around her was suddenly full of mermaids.

The little mermaid was clinging to her mother's hair.

Who's that with her?

She's back!

Then Mairi felt the rock beneath her feet and she could stand.

The little mermaid was telling everyone her story. 'Look what the crab did to my tail,' she said.

'Maybe it'll teach you not to go off like that,' said her mother. 'I've told you and told you. If it hadn't have been for this girl.' She smiled at Mairi. 'How can we ever thank you?' she said.

Mairi shook the crab!

And Mairi had a sudden idea.

'You couldn't teach me how to swim, could you?' she asked. 'I mean, like you do, like mermaids do.'

First they taught her how to lie on the water and float. Mairi could feel the water holding her up!

Doggy paddle was next . . .

then breaststroke . . .

then crawl . . .

backstroke .

butterfly . . .

They even taught her to swim underwater!

Mairi wasn't afraid of the sea anymore.

She loved it!

Some time later Robbie was waiting for
the next really big wave to come in,
waiting for just the right one to dive into.
'Look at this one!' he cried as a great
green wave came curling in.

He was just about to dive into it when he

saw what looked like a seal swimming

along the crest of the wave

But it wasn't a seal, it was Mairi. It was

Mairi swimming!

As she swept past him, his mouth opened

in astonishment and the seawater swept in.

'You can swim!' he spluttered.

Mairi's mother and father came running

down to the water's edge.

'You can swim!' they cried.

'Course I can,' she said. 'It's easy.

I just pretended I was a mermaid.'